Glamour!

Stardom!

Fame and fortune

could be one step away!

Welcome to

Fame School

For another fix of

read

Rising Star

Secret Ambition

Rivals!

Tara's Triumph

Lucky Break

Solo Star

Christmas Stars

Coming soon...

Pop Diva

Fame School

Reach for the Stars

Cindy Jefferies

USBORNE

Thanks to Rebecca and Gavin Landless for all
their wonderful performances, Elle for the magazines
and advice, and everyone at Usborne for working so hard
to make this series the best it could be.

For
Maria McKnight
1896-1914

First published in 2005 by Usborne Publishing Ltd., Usborne House,
83-85 Saffron Hill, London EC1N 8RT, England. www.usborne.com

Copyright © 2005 by Cindy Jefferies. The right of Cindy Jefferies to be identified
as the author of this work has been asserted by her in accordance with the
Copyright, Designs and Patents Act, 1988.

The name Usborne and the devices ♀ ⊕ are Trade Marks of
Usborne Publishing Ltd.

All rights reserved. No part of this publication may be reproduced, stored
in a retrieval system or transmitted in any form or by any means, electronic, mechanical,
photocopying, recording or otherwise without the prior
permission of the publisher.

This is a work of fiction. The characters, incidents, and dialogues are products of the
author's imagination and are not to be construed as real. Any resemblance to actual events
or persons, living or dead, is entirely coincidental.

A CIP catalogue record for this book is available from the British Library.

FMAMJJASOND/07

ISBN 9780746061176

Printed in India.

1 Born to Sing

Chloe stood alone, a small figure in black jeans and a pink top. As the music began, she was almost completely still, with her arms loosely at her sides, only one heel moving slightly to the beat. Her pixie face, topped by her trademark, tousled brown hair seemed tiny in front of the massive speakers. Camera Two was swooping down behind her, filming the vast crowd of people swaying to the intro. But Chloe was totally focused. Her fans, and the song, deserved everything from her.

She turned to where she knew Camera One was waiting. At once her face appeared in close-up on the huge screen behind her. A collective sigh went up from her audience. She raised the microphone reverently, close to her mouth. The first lines were delivered softly, pleadingly, and then, halfway through the first verse, the power of the song took over.

Her face was full of emotion, and in her mind her voice soared, filling the vast auditorium with pure sound. She was looking right into the camera, opening her heart for everyone at home, as well as those who had come to the concert. The crowd was rapt, totally in her hands. She was giving the performance of her life.

"Chloe, can I borrow this?" Jess was holding up a pale blue Indian scarf. Camera, stage, crowd, everything vanished.

Chloe stood for a second, trying to bring back the imagined performance, but the moment had gone. It was no use. Jess had barged right in front of the mirror before Chloe had finished miming to it. She put her hairbrush down gently, as if it really were a microphone.

"I hadn't finished," she told Jess, feeling the last wisps of her audience dissolve to nothing. "And it's important how you sing to a camera. D'you know, I read in a magazine that when you're famous you have to make the camera your friend."

"Sorry." Jess was Chloe's best friend, but even she couldn't see what Chloe was imagining, or hear the song that she was singing inside her head. "Is there still going to be room to dance now you've got this desk in your room?" she asked.

Chloe took a hard look at the offending homework desk her mum had insisted on buying. There had been little enough floor space before.

"Let's go for it. We'll do the dance we practised. Don't forget, it's step turn, step turn." They lined up together and Chloe started the music with the volume turned well down. The thumping beat needed to be louder, but she didn't want to risk getting into trouble for waking her little brother.

"Is it Ben's bedtime already?" Jess asked. Chloe nodded. Step turn, step turn, step—

"Ow!" Chloe stumbled against the desk and sent her homework flying.

"When I'm famous," she told Jess crossly, "I'm going to have a *huge* bedroom. In fact, I'll probably have one room to sleep in and another just for my clothes and stuff. I certainly won't bother with a desk! I won't copy other people's dances either. Someone will make them up to go with the songs I sing. *And* I'll have proper clothes for my performances," she added, draping a remnant of curtain material over her shoulder before tossing it onto her bed in despair.

"Cool," said Jess. "You can get anything you want when you're famous. I'm going to have a hundred kittens in my dressing room."

"A hundred kittens would be far too many!" said Chloe. She knew Jess only mentioned kittens because her mum wouldn't let her have one of Katie Wilson's. "Imagine all the puddles on the carpet," she added, wrinkling her nose.

"One of my servants could mop them up," Jess giggled.

Chloe sighed, rubbing the bruise on her bum. "Being famous isn't just about being rich, you know," she said. "It's not a game, Jess. I know it's fun dreaming about loads of money, and having what we want, but it's more than that! I really want to *be* a pop singer, not just dream about it. Imagine making thousands of people happy when you sing. Wouldn't that be amazing? That's what I want to do, but we'll never make it if you don't take it seriously."

"I *am* taking it seriously!"

Step turn, step turn. There was just room between the desk, the dressing table and Chloe's bed. Chloe nudged Jess and they raised their microphones together for the final line of the song. Jess's voice rang out in the tiny room before she remembered about Ben. Chloe dived for the CD player, but it was too late.

"What on earth are you doing?"

They both started guiltily. "Nothing."

Chloe's mum was standing in the doorway. She looked really cross.

"Well you've disturbed Ben again. How many times have I told you to keep quiet while he gets off to sleep?

You know if he hears your voices he wants to get back out of bed."

"Sorry," they mumbled.

"Have you finished your homework?" Chloe's mum had noticed the fallen school books.

"Not yet."

"I thought that's why you were both up here. Honestly Chloe, if you started your homework as soon as I put Ben to bed you wouldn't keep him awake, would you?"

Chloe shook her head.

"Perhaps I ought to go," Jess said awkwardly.

"Well, maybe that would be a good idea," Chloe's mum agreed. "While Ben's going through this difficult stage it would be better if you came round straight after school instead of after tea."

The girls walked soberly downstairs together. "Sorry about that," Jess whispered. "See you tomorrow." She shimmied down the front path and out of the gate without a care in the world.

Chloe closed the front door and leaned up against it.

It was all right for Jess. She didn't have a little brother who wouldn't go to sleep, or a stupid desk in the way of dancing practice, *and* Jess's mum wasn't always nagging her to do her homework. She wished she were allowed to go to Jess's house more often. It was so hard, thought Chloe, to keep her ambition alive when the rest of her family didn't care about her making it as a singer. And Jess didn't have to keep her voice down all the time.

Chloe dawdled back up the stairs, deep in thought. The memory still burned in her of the birthday party years ago when everyone had laughed at the way she'd sung *Happy Birthday*. Even now, she was certain she hadn't been out of tune, just loud.

Even worse, when she had sung in the choir at primary school, Mrs. Pendle had constantly been at her to pipe down because her voice didn't fit in with the rest of the class. It wasn't fair.

Mum was waiting for her on the landing. "Now," she said. "You'd better clear up this mess and get on with your homework. I don't know what those books are doing on the floor. You should take more care of them. They're important."

"You didn't have to tell me off in front of Jess," Chloe said angrily, slapping the books back onto her desk. "It was embarrassing."

"Well, I'm sorry, but if you'd been quietly doing your homework there wouldn't have· been a problem. Besides, you're at secondary school now. You're growing up. You can't spend all your time with Jess pretending to be a pop singer. I've told you before how important it is to make a good impression at your new school. You don't want the teachers to give up on you."

"Fine!" Chloe closed her bedroom door behind her, resisting the urge to slam it. She slumped onto the chair in front of her new desk and leaned her chin on her hands.

She wouldn't give up. She wouldn't! No matter how difficult Mum made it. One day, she and Jess would be up there on the telly for everyone to see. *Then* her mum wouldn't go on about homework!

2 A Chance to Shine?

Chloe and Jess drifted along the corridor eating their crisps. They still hadn't got used to their new school yet. Beacon Comp was so big and noisy compared to their primary school. The buildings were old, and the walls needed painting. Chloe wondered if she'd ever feel at home here.

"Break's boring when it's raining," she grumbled to Jess, brushing bits of crisp off her jumper. She dropped the packet into a bin and licked her fingers.

"Come and read this, then," Jess said. "Look! They're going to do *Bugsy Malone*!" There was a piece of bright red paper pinned to a notice board. The writing was inside a large, splat-shaped border.

"*Lower-school pupils who want to be in* Bugsy Malone *should come for an audition in the hall on Thursday,*" Chloe read out.

"Remember, we watched the video ages ago?" said Jess. "All those kids playing gangsters, with splat guns and custard pies?"

"*We* ought to go to the audition," said Chloe.

"It's not *pop* singing," said Jess critically.

"But we've never been to an audition," Chloe said. "It would be good experience for later on when we audition for one of those pop star TV shows."

"Oh! Okay," said Jess, easily convinced. "I suppose you're right. We might have real microphones and everything!" She rummaged in her bag for a pen. "I'll put our names on the list. There!" She scrawled their names on the paper, under several others. "Come on, I want to go to the loo before maths."

"I'll catch you up," said Chloe. Once Jess had gone, she looked at the notice again. It *would* be a good idea to go to an audition, but she wasn't sure she actually wanted a part. They might get to be in the chorus, and she'd have to remember to sing quietly or everyone would complain. On the other hand, perhaps she *couldn't* sing loudly any more. It was ages since she'd really let rip. Mrs. Pendle had put a stop to all that.

Part of her wanted to scrub her name out. What if they went along and everybody laughed at her? Perhaps it would be better if she told Jess she'd changed her mind.

But what if I did audition and got a big part, and someone important like a talent scout came to see the show?

It *could* happen. Someone in this huge school *might* have a relation who was in the music industry. Oh! And if they came to the show and liked her voice, they might sign her up, straight away! But if she didn't even *audition*, she'd have no chance.

The bell rang for the next lesson and Chloe made her way down the corridor. Hordes of kids were streaming past in both directions. She had to hold her bag in front of her to stop it being pulled off her shoulder in the crush.

If she and Jess went to the audition, and people laughed, she'd *die*. But maybe, if she sang quietly, it wouldn't be so bad. And if she could get the video of *Bugsy Malone* and learn some of the songs really well, that would give her an edge. Yes! Get the video. Learn the songs. Make it so they *had* to give her a solo part. And Jess, of course.

But Jess wasn't interested in learning the songs.

"That's daft," she said, leading the way home after school. "We could spend ages learning a song for nothing. It's only a school thing, Chloe. It's not *that* important."

"But..."

"I can't come round this afternoon, anyway. I promised my mum I'd go shopping with her."

"We've only got tonight to practise, Jess! And I've got the video out of the school library now. Come round after shopping, then." But Jess shook her head.

"What about your brother? We'd only get told off again. *You* watch it," she added, seeing Chloe's disappointed face. "You learn a song tonight, then you can teach it to me in the morning on the way to school. Don't worry! We'll blag our way through the audition. It'll be a laugh."

"Yeah, right."

Chloe ran up the path and indoors. If they were going for this audition she was determined to do it properly. It might only be a school production, but it was a start.

As she had expected, Ben was in front of the telly, watching one of his videos with great attention.

"Look, Ben!" Chloe coaxed, taking the *Bugsy* video out of her bag. "I've got a new one. We can watch it together." Ben looked suspiciously at the box.

"Want my one," he said doubtfully.

"In a minute," Chloe said. "It's my turn now."

For a few minutes, Ben sat on his sister's lap and watched, but he soon started to fidget. He scrambled down and toddled over to the telly.

"Want *my* one."

Chloe rewound the tape and listened to the first song again. Ben was pushing his video in front of her face.

"Ben! I'm trying to watch this. Play with your car for a bit."

"Want *my* one, Co-ee!" He was starting to get upset. Chloe glared at her little brother. She loved him dearly, but sometimes he could be a right pain. And this was *important*.

At last he scooted off on his car and Chloe rewound the tape again. She was beginning to get the words now, and the tune wasn't difficult, but then she heard her mum calling.

"What?" she yelled back. "I'll come in a minute."

"Could you put Ben's video on for him, Chloe?" her mum repeated. "I'm trying to hem some curtains and I can't do it with Ben under my feet. Can't you play with him a bit?" she added, coming into the sitting room. "He hasn't seen you all day. What are you watching?" Chloe had turned the sound down, but the kids on the video were still strutting their stuff.

"It's *Bugsy Malone*. I borrowed it from the school library."

"Well, maybe you can watch it later, or at the

weekend," Mum said. "Let him watch his video now. It won't be that long before he's in bed." She swapped the videos and Ben climbed back happily onto his sister's lap.

"*My* one," he told her, wriggling excitedly.

It was *so* unfair. *Everything* was stacked against this audition. Chloe felt as if she was totally invisible. What about what *she* wanted?

Ben didn't need her. Soon he was totally absorbed in the cartoon. Chloe eased him off her lap and onto the chair. She went up to her room and stared into the mirror. Her face looked back miserably. She must never let her fans see her like this.

She closed her eyes and tried to think herself into being Chloe the pop diva, but when she opened them again she was still plain Chloe Tompkins in a navy school jumper.

She couldn't blag her way through the audition like Jess said. She wanted to do it properly, professionally. It meant everything to her. Tomorrow *could* lead to something really big.

3 A Good Day Ends Badly

Chloe kept telling herself not to be nervous at the audition, but that was easier said than done. Jess was fine. But then Jess didn't really care if she got a part or not. Chloe *did* care. She'd spent half the night worrying about it. Having decided that there was a possibility, however small, that *someone* might recognize her talent if she ·got a part, she really had to go for it. But her family didn't make it easy.

It hadn't always been like that. When Chloe was little, her mum used to find her fun things to dress up in so she could pretend to be a pop star on TV. Her mum and dad loved listening to her sing, then. But now she was at secondary school, her mum seemed to think that being a pop singer wasn't a proper career option any more. She got cross when Chloe went on about it, so Jess was the only person Chloe could confide in.

And Jess was sworn to secrecy. None of Chloe's other friends knew anything about her ambition. She didn't want people to think she was showing off. And she didn't want people feeling sorry for her if she failed.

She *had* to do well at the audition. She couldn't fail the first time she tried. It would be too awful.

As it turned out, it didn't matter about the video. They didn't have to perform songs at the audition. Instead, Mr. Watkins, the music teacher, made them sing scales, accompanied by the piano. Chloe was so nervous she kept her voice really quiet, so quiet that Mr. Watkins made her go through the scales twice. He made her sing much higher and quite a bit lower than the others too.

"You ought to join the choir," he said. Chloe blushed. That was the *last* thing she wanted to hear. Even if people *didn't* get cross about her voice standing out in this school choir, it was the wrong sort of singing. You had to sing all sorts of crummy songs and make your face sort of wobble when you reached the high notes. There was a famous girl on telly who sang that way and she was always on programmes for old people. That was not what Chloe wanted at all.

"Okay. Let's have a bit of hush," said Mr. Watkins, when everyone had sung their scales and had started chattering. "Thank you all for coming. It's especially good to see some of the new year sevens turning up." Jess grinned at Chloe, but she was too nervous to smile back.

"I try to give the main parts to years eight and nine in lower-school productions and I have some strong contenders here. Now, let's get you sorted out." Mr. Watkins pulled out several older children and made them stand together by the piano. Then he sent a larger group over to the window. Chloe and Jess were in this group. A few children were left in the middle and Mr. Watkins spoke to them first.

"I'd like you to be involved backstage," he told them. "There's lots you can do. Costumes, scenery, props.

A Good Day Ends Badly

These are all vital jobs. Mr. Thomas here will take you into room G2 so you can discuss who is to do what. Okay?"

Jess nudged Chloe. "They can't sing," she whispered with a giggle. A couple of older children in their group glared at her and she shut up.

"You," said Mr. Watkins to the group at the piano, "will play the main parts. I'll come back to you in a moment."

There were grins and sighs of relief all round in the piano group. But Chloe held her breath. Her group had to be the chorus. They just had to be.

"You lot," continued Mr. Watkins, spreading his arms wide, "will be the chorus."

Chloe let her breath go. Yes! She'd got in. Although she would have far preferred having a solo part, even the best pop singers have to start somewhere, and at least she was going to sing onstage.

"First rehearsal for the chorus will be next Wednesday lunchtime in the music room. So you lot can scoot off now. Well done, all of you. See you next week!"

As they pushed their way into the corridor, Chloe felt her heart soaring crazily. She fizzed with excitement. No one had laughed at her voice! Mr. Watkins had even seemed to like it. Okay, so she hadn't been given a proper part, but that wasn't her fault. It was only because she was a year seven. It was a start, a good start.

Later on, when she got home from school that afternoon, Chloe fell in through the front door still full of enthusiasm.

"Guess what!" she announced, tossing her school bag onto the hall floor and rushing into the kitchen. "I went to an audition today and I'm in *Bugsy Malone*! Jess is in it as well, and the first rehearsal is next Wednesday!"

Her mum smiled. "Stop prancing around and tell me properly," she said. "And mind Ben's crayons. There are some on the floor."

"I was really nervous," Chloe said, stooping to pick up the wax crayons. "We had to do scales to show we could sing okay and I *could*! In fact I sang higher than anyone. I sang lower too. It was brilliant! Mr. Watkins said I should join the school choir, but I'm not sure I want to do that."

"What is it you want to be in?"

"Not *want*," corrected Chloe. "I *am* in it. *Bugsy Malone*. You know. I got the video out of the library yesterday. I thought I would have to learn songs for the audition but it was all right. I didn't need to."

"Well done for the audition," Mum said. "But shouldn't you have asked us first?" Chloe stared at her mother.

"Why? Mr. Watkins was really pleased that some year sevens had turned up."

"I'm sure he was, but he's a music teacher, isn't he? What would your maths teacher think?"

"What do you mean?" Chloe was getting a bit fed up. She had been in a brilliant mood when she'd come home, but now Mum was spoiling everything. "It's nothing to do with my maths teacher."

"Well," Mum was filling the kettle and plugging it in, "you'll have to learn lines, go to rehearsals, take part in the production. All that takes time. I know what you're like. You'll get so carried away that you'll skimp even more on your homework."

"I *won't!*" Chloe slumped down at the kitchen table. "You wanted me to settle in at my new school. Well, this *is* settling in. I have to take part. I got chosen. And I really *want* to do it. It's important."

Chloe's heart was beating almost as fast as it had before the audition. Surely her mum wouldn't stop her being in *Bugsy*? She *couldn't.* It would be too mean. Besides, this was the beginning of her career. She couldn't bear it if Jess got noticed and she didn't, all because her mum hadn't let her take part. That would be too awful. It was hard enough to break into the music industry without her *mum* holding her back. She had to take every chance she got, even if it was only a school production.

"Mum." She put her hand on her mum's arm. "I'll be really good at doing my homework. I'll work extra hard at my maths. I won't let rehearsals take up too much time. I'll do *anything*." She swallowed. "I won't let Jess come round after school. We'll only practise at weekends. *Please!*"

Her mum gave her a quick hug. "I don't want to be mean, Chloe. And I am really pleased for you that you got chosen. But I do worry about your schoolwork. You and Jess go round with your heads in the clouds most of the time."

Chloe took a deep breath. Mum would *never* say yes if Chloe started a row. She had to keep her temper at all costs.

I was nervous, but I got through the audition. Surely she's not going to stop me now? Oh, what can I say to make her agree?

Mum looked at Chloe's stricken face and sighed.

"Well, we'll see what Dad thinks when he comes home, but *I* don't think being in a musical is a very good idea at all."

4 The Letter

Parents can make life *so* difficult sometimes. But luckily Chloe's dad wasn't too concerned about her being in *Bugsy*.

"It would be different if she had a major part," he said. "But I don't think being in the chorus will matter too much. She might even try a bit more at her schoolwork because she's grateful we've let her take part!"

Chloe nodded. "I told Mum I would," she agreed hastily.

"Well, okay," said Mum. "But make sure you don't forget about *your* side of the bargain. And you'd better find out when the performance is. I'll get a babysitter sorted out for Ben."

The Letter

Chloe threw herself into the rehearsals for *Bugsy*. They were really good fun, even though being in musicals wasn't *quite* what she had in mind for a career. At least she was onstage, and singing too. With her voice carefully under control, no one complained. She even remembered to get her homework done on time, and she and Jess restricted their pop sessions to the weekends, mostly.

"I got eight out of ten for my maths test today," Chloe told her parents happily on Friday evening, while Ben was being bathed. "Mrs. Bardley was really pleased. Oh! And I forgot. There's a letter from school for you in my bag." She dodged into her room and rummaged for the letter. "Mr. Watkins said he might let me sing one line solo in *Bugsy*!" she yelled from her room.

"Well done, times two!" Mum said when Chloe reappeared at the bathroom door.

"That's a good maths result," said Dad. "What's this letter about?" he added, winding up another of Ben's bath toys. Chloe handed the letter to Mum because she had dry hands.

"Don't know," Chloe said. "We all got them."

Chloe's mum leaned against the sink, reading the letter. "Oh no!" she sighed.

"What?" asked Chloe. Her mum handed her the letter rather reluctantly and Chloe looked at it. At the top was a small picture of a big house, like a stately home, and just underneath were the words Rockley Park in large black and red writing.

Rockley Park is a school for aspiring popular singers, songwriters and musicians, she read. *The school is pleased to be able to offer two scholarship places to pupils of Beacon Comprehensive School. Places can be taken up in years seven, ten or twelve. Applications for scholarships must be in by September 10th to qualify for the term beginning October 3rd.*

Chloe had never heard of Rockley Park. She hadn't realized that there was such a thing as a school for aspiring popular singers. Surely that meant pop singers? Didn't it? Anyway, why would they want to offer places to people at *her* school? It didn't make sense. It must be a mistake. Oh! But if only it wasn't!

She picked up the envelope and looked inside. There was another piece of paper that Mum had missed.

"Here," Chloe said, holding it out. Her hand was shaking.

"Calm down," said Mum. As if that was possible.

"What?" asked Dad. "What is it?" Mum read the second letter and handed it to Chloe.

"Read it to your father," she said flatly.

"*Dear parent,*" Chloe began. "*I enclose an offer we have been sent by the popular music school at Rockley Park. This unusual situation has come about because one of the benefactors of Rockley Park attended our school and now wishes to encourage any promising pupils by offering two free residential places at the respected music school.*" The letter was trembling in her hand so much that Chloe was having trouble reading it.

"For goodness' sake!" grumbled Mum. She took the letter back. "*I should point out that the school exists to train highly talented youngsters and demands a great deal of commitment. If your child wishes to* apply... blah blah... *they ought to see Mr. Watkins without delay as time is very short,*" read Mum briskly, before tossing the letter onto the windowsill.

"Well, that will get all the silliest girls rushing round to Mr. Watkins first thing on Monday morning!" Dad said. "I bet no boys apply!"

Chloe was still trembling. How could her dad laugh? Didn't he realize what an amazing opportunity this was?

Chloe had thought it was vital that she performed in *Bugsy*, but this letter changed all that. This was a way of getting straight to where she wanted to be, right in the music industry, or at least close to it!

Famous people often spoke about their Big Chance. When the original star was ill and they took over the part, or they overheard something important that won them a role, or it was a mistake but they got to shine anyway and from then on they were famous. This could be it, better than any school production. Chloe's Big Chance!

She looked from Dad, splashing Ben in the bath, to Mum, leaning against the sink.

"What do I have to do?" she asked in a small voice. "How do I apply?"

"Don't even think about it," said Mum briskly. She took a towel off the rail and lifted Ben out. Dad got to his feet and rubbed Chloe's hair with his wet hand. "*You're* not a silly girl," he said fondly.

Chloe grabbed the letter, went into her room and closed the door. She couldn't sit down, or do anything. She was so agitated her whole body was shaking. She had to apply. She just had to. She and Jess could win the places and go to Rockley Park. They'd learn how to be pop singers and become really successful. Then her parents wouldn't laugh. She *had* to convince them, somehow.

"It did say *free* places," she told them a few minutes later, putting her head round Ben's bedroom door.

"The school you're at is free," Dad said.

Later, when Ben was in bed and she had her parents all to herself, she tried again. "I don't think you realize how important this is to me," she said, trying to sound reasonable. "It's what I *really* want to do."

"It says that the school demands a lot of commitment," Dad reminded her. "That means hard work, Chloe, not something you're very good at."

"But this is what I want to do for a *job,*" she insisted. "Of *course* I'll work hard at something I really want!"

"But you only see the people who are *successful* on television," Mum said. "For every one of those there are probably thousands who never get anywhere. Being a pop singer is a huge gamble. You should be growing out of that sort of daydreaming, and start focusing on a sensible career, like teaching."

"I *won't* grow out of it," said Chloe. She was getting desperate. Her voice was wobbling, and she was near to tears. "It's my Big Chance. You're always telling me to be ambitious and aim high because you wasted *your* chance at college. Well I *am* aiming high. And now I *have* a chance, and you won't let me go for it." Her mum's face tightened, and Chloe could see she had gone too far. There was going to be an almighty argument.

"Hang on," said Dad. "What does it say about applying? Is it very involved? Where's the letter?"

"Here," said Chloe, pulling it from her pocket. She handed it back to her mum.

"It says the school will record applicants and send the recordings to Rockley Park," Mum said coldly, scanning the letter.

"If we let you do that," said Dad. "Will you be satisfied? Will that make you happy?" Chloe couldn't speak. She nodded. "Well then," Dad said to Mum, "let her do this recording thing and send it in. Hopefully it'll get it out of her system, and at least she won't be able to accuse us of not letting her try." He turned to her again. "Does that sound fair, Chloe?"

"Will that be an end to it if we let you do that?" Mum asked.

Chloe could see herself on that stage already, the microphone poised in her hand.

No. Of course it won't be an end to it. I'll never, ever want to give up.

She had never felt so excited, but she arranged her face into a quiet, grateful shape.

"Of course it will," she agreed. "Of course."

5 Chloe's Big Chance

"We'll do our favourite song," Jess told Chloe while walking to school on Monday morning. She didn't have any problems with *her* mum. She let Jess do whatever she liked. "I hope Mr. Watkins has got a good karaoke. Let's run. If we're quick we can go and see him before first lesson!"

But Mr. Watkins didn't have any sort of karaoke in the music department, and Jess was appalled. "It'll sound pants!" she muttered to Chloe when it was obvious he expected them to perform with him playing the piano. He wouldn't let them make a recording together either.

"You can't apply as a duo," he told them. "Rockley

Chloe's Big Chance

Park wants to hear individuals, not groups. Now, who's going to go first?"

"Me!" Jess stepped forward. After a few attempts, Mr. Watkins could play the song well enough for Jess to sing along. She was word perfect, but couldn't stop giggling. They had to go through it several times before they got a good recording.

Chloe watched and listened carefully. It wasn't exactly pants with the piano, but neither was it very professional. Jess was doing all the moves really brilliantly, as if she were onstage, but she wasn't being filmed, so none of the dancing would count. It was scary. Chloe's only chance was to get everything of the performance onto the recording. But how was she supposed to do that? If only it was a video. But they were in their school uniforms so that wouldn't work either. It was agony, trying to think how to do it. It was much worse than the audition for *Bugsy*.

"Right, Chloe. Your turn." In a daze, Chloe took Jess's place next to the piano. "Are you sure you want to sing the same song?" asked Mr. Watkins. Chloe wasn't sure about *anything.* She tried to think herself into her bedroom mirror, where her audience waited. Jess was nodding at her furiously.

"Yes," she said. She sang it without the movements she and Jess had practised in her room. She knew she sang it too quietly, but she couldn't help that. She imagined herself giving it the full treatment and hoped some of that emotion would come through.

"Well done," said Mr. Watkins. "Now, do you mind singing some scales as well? It's important to show what you can do, and that song doesn't show off your range."

"What's range?" she asked. Jess was giggling again, but Chloe ignored her. Mr. Watkins was a music teacher after all. He *might* know what was best.

"It's how high and how low you can comfortably sing," he explained. "Some people are good at going very high or quite low, but your voice is unusual because you can do both. You can sing the high notes *and* lots of low notes too."

He told Chloe to concentrate on hitting each note as

accurately as she could. He made her do them loads of times, and they got the recording finished just before the bell went for the first lesson.

"I don't know why you agreed to do those scales," Jess grumbled as they raced off to English. "You want to be a pop singer, not some silly opera person. If you're not careful, you'll get chosen for the wrong thing." She was a bit miffed because Mr. Watkins hadn't asked her to sing any scales. Even so, Chloe was concerned that Jess might be right.

Mr. Watkins promised to send the recordings and application forms to Rockley Park straight away. So all they could do now was wait. But waiting was awful, however much they concentrated on the *Bugsy* rehearsals. Learning dances for the musical as well as the songs was a good laugh. And they were going to get proper costumes. But nothing, absolutely nothing, took away the agony of waiting.

"Who else applied for a place?" Chloe asked Jess for the hundredth time.

"*I* don't know," her friend snapped, rolling off

Chloe's bed and checking her hair in the mirror. "Mr. Watkins wouldn't tell us, would he?"

"I bet that girl in the upper school has applied," Chloe fretted. "You know, the one who played the saxophone in assembly last week. She was brilliant. It's not just singers they're looking for either. We don't stand a chance against someone like her."

"There was a rumour going round that a year-twelve boy applied," Jess said.

"Isn't he supposed to be in a rock band?" Chloe asked. "I think he might be the one with long black hair. Darren something."

"That's right," Jess agreed, rummaging amongst Chloe's hairbands. "I think he plays lead guitar." They looked at each other dejectedly. How could they possibly compete with someone who already played guitar in a rock band? All *they* did was mess about in Chloe's bedroom.

"What clothes do you think they wear at Rockley Park?" Jess asked, trying to keep their spirits up. But Chloe didn't have the heart for it any more. She could feel her Big Chance slipping away from her, each day that went by.

Why hadn't they heard? Had Rockley Park lost the recordings? Did they only reply to people who had won places? That would be too cruel. Worst of all, how could she bear it if Jess got in and she didn't?

Chloe knew she ought to forget all about it and get on with her life. After all, she was in *Bugsy*, wasn't she? And Mr. Watkins had given her not one, but two whole lines to sing solo. A couple of weeks ago she had been thrilled about that, now it seemed meaningless compared to getting into Rockley Park.

Chloe joined Jess and they stared into the mirror together. Jess pulled a face at Chloe's miserable expression. She reached a finger to Chloe's reflected mouth and drew a smeary smile onto the glass.

"Come on," she said. "It's not that bad." But it *was* that bad. Chloe knew she would *die* if she didn't get in.

6 A Bit of a Shock

No one could stay as strung out as Chloe was and keep going. However much she willed good news to arrive, even *she* started to let go of the dream a little. Life got in the way, and she was busy, what with schoolwork, and *Bugsy*, and looking forward to half term. So when the letter finally *did* arrive, she wasn't ready for it.

One afternoon she came home from school late because of a *Bugsy* rehearsal. She was pleased but surprised to see her dad there in the kitchen, drinking tea with Mum. He was hardly ever home early.

"Come and sit down," Mum said, once Chloe had hung up her coat.

A Bit of a Shock

"But I've got masses of homework," Chloe objected. "And I want to watch telly later."

She didn't get it, even though her dad was there and her mum was giving her funny looks. Chloe was thinking more about her favourite TV programme than what Mum and Dad might want.

"Sit down for a moment," Dad said, patting a kitchen chair. "We've got something to talk about." He picked up the letter that was lying on the table.

Chloe dumped her bag on the floor. For a fleeting moment she wondered if she'd done something really wrong at school and if her form tutor had written to complain. She couldn't think of anything, but her parents were acting so oddly. There must be something wrong. Ben was there, playing on the floor, so it couldn't be anything to do with him. Her brain insisted on working at half speed, even when she noticed the letter in her dad's hand. Slowly it dawned on her. It must be *the* letter. The one she'd almost-but-not-quite given up on. Time stood still.

. It was important not to be upset in front of them.

She'd promised not to mind.

"It's all right," she gabbled, trying not to feel anything. "I don't mind. I won't be miserable. Honestly."

"You'd better read it," said Mum quietly.

"Well, go on," insisted Dad, holding it out. Chloe didn't want to. What was the point? But she had to take it, and slide the thick expensive paper out of its envelope.

Rockley Park School would like your daughter Chloe Tompkins to attend an interview and audition on September 21st at 2 p.m...

She couldn't get any further. Her eyes kept going over the same sentence again and again.

"It doesn't mean you have to go," said Dad.

Chloe looked up. "What do you mean?" She put the wild imaginings running through her head to one side. "I've got an interview and audition. I *have* to go. You can't stop me."

"We don't know anything about this place, Chloe," said Mum. "What is the standard of teaching like? Do they teach any sensible subjects, or is it all pop nonsense? And it's a *boarding* school. You couldn't come home every day and tell us all your troubles. What if you were unhappy?"

Chloe couldn't believe how unfair they were being.

"Why did you let me apply if you thought it was such an awful place?" she demanded. Her dad looked embarrassed.

"To be honest, love, we didn't think you'd get an audition. It never occurred to us that you would."

"Well, I showed you then, didn't I!" She was angry, really angry. How dare they assume she was no good? She'd got an *interview*, and an *audition*!

"I'm sorry," said Mum. "But education is important." She tried to give Chloe a hug, but Chloe shrugged her off.

"You can't stop me from going," she said. "I've earned that audition, all by myself. You should be proud of me." She almost let out a sob at that, but held up her head and bit it back.

"Oh, Chloe." Her dad sighed. "We *are* proud of you. We're just worried. We don't know anything about this sort of thing."

Chloe could see that they'd *never* say yes unless they found out more about the school.

"Go and see Mr. Watkins," Chloe told them, determined not to give up. "He's still at school sorting out one of the solos for *Bugsy*. He'll tell you. He knows all about it. I think he's even been there once!" She willed them to agree. "Please."

Dad looked at Mum. "We can't interrupt him in the middle of rehearsals," he said doubtfully.

Chloe looked at her watch. "He'll be finished in half an hour. We can go then." She tried to sound serious, and sensible.

Mum sighed. "Mrs. Robbins might be able to look after Ben," she said. "I'll go and ask her." She got up and went next door. Chloe could feel herself starting to fizz with excitement and fought the feeling down. Surely Mr. Watkins would be on her side?

They caught the music teacher at the end of rehearsals. He took them into his tiny office and found chairs for her parents, while Chloe leaned against a shelf piled high with books and papers.

"Rockley Park is a proper school," Mr. Watkins told them, once he'd congratulated Chloe. "The children work very hard because they have to fit in the extra classes in singing, dance, songwriting and music technology amongst a full timetable of curriculum subjects. It's by no means an easy option. Why don't you take the prospectus and see what you think?" He handed a glossy brochure to Chloe's mum with *Welcome to Rockley Park School for the Performing Arts* on the cover.

"What do you think the school saw in Chloe?" asked Dad.

"Well... " Mr. Watkins smiled. "I suspect it was her range." Chloe hugged the information to herself. Those scales *had* been worth it after all. "She has quite an unusual voice," he went on. "It's not particularly strong, but training would help with that. She's got excellent pitch, and can sing an amazing range of notes. I should think that's what interested them. If it's what she wants to do, this is a fantastic opportunity for her," he added.

"It's what I really, really want," Chloe assured everyone. Mr. Watkins laughed.

"There you go, a girl with real ambition and determination!" he said. "And she'll need every bit of it if she goes into the music industry! My advice," he went on more soberly, "is to go along when she has her interview and see for yourselves. I went to a concert there last year and was most impressed with the whole set up."

"Is there anything in particular she should do before she goes?" asked Dad. Chloe's heart gave a great leap in her chest.

Yes! Dad's going to let me do it!

"Come and practise every lunchtime before you go," he said. "You need to be as polished as possible for the audition."

Chloe nodded excitedly. Then she remembered Jess. "Who else has got an interview?" she asked anxiously.

Mr. Watkins smiled. "I have the list here," he said. "There are a few other children going, but only one other person in your year has been called for audition."

A Bit of a Shock

Chloe breathed out a huge, triumphant breath. It was better than she could ever have hoped for. It was going to be just as they had planned.

"The other person," she blurted out, her eyes shining with pleasure and excitement. "It's Jess, isn't it!"

7. A Broken Friendship

Chloe was bubbling over with excitement. Back home, her parents were finally beginning to see things her way! Her mum kept reading bits out of the prospectus, and sounded more and more approving by the minute.

"Lots of opportunities in the industry apart from performing, and many of our students go on to university," she told Chloe in a pleased voice. Well, fine. Let her stick to her dream of higher education for Chloe if she wanted. Chloe had more important things on her mind. She had to phone Jess.

Because Jess *hadn't* got an interview after all. The other person who was going from Chloe's year was a boy, Danny James, and he wasn't even a singer.

He played the drums, for goodness' sake!

Chloe didn't know what to say to Jess. In the end she bottled out, and didn't call her that evening. It was too difficult. She hoped it might be easier to tell her face to face on the way to school in the morning. But it wasn't. Jess was furious, and very hurt.

"Fancy you knowing about it straight after school and not telling me," she wailed. "The *least* a best friend would have done was phone. Then I would have had the chance to get used to the idea. *Everyone* knows we were both going for places. It's going to be *horrible* at school for me today." She was right, and Chloe felt terrible.

"I won't tell anyone," she offered. "No one need know. I probably won't get in anyway."

"But I'm *definitely* not getting in, am I?" Jess stumped on ahead and Chloe trailed behind, lost for words.

It would be difficult, but Chloe decided that for Jess's sake she definitely wouldn't tell anyone at school her news today. Perhaps Jess would feel better tomorrow. But Chloe knew how terrible she would have felt if Jess had got the interview instead of her.

As it turned out, there was no chance to keep it secret anyway. Their tutor announced Chloe's news before he took the register, and from then on people kept coming up to her and asking about it, even kids older than her, and teachers she didn't know.

At break, Chloe was surrounded by lots of excited kids and Jess was nowhere to be seen. For the rest of the day, Jess went round with a different group, and Chloe didn't get the chance to speak to her. After school, Chloe found herself walking home alone.

The next morning she waited for Jess to call for her, but she didn't turn up. It got later and later, and in the end Chloe had to run all the way to school, and was still late. Jess was already in class. And she wouldn't look when Chloe tried to catch her eye. It was terrible. All this time they should have been together, planning what to wear for their visit to Rockley Park. But every time Chloe thought about the coming trip and felt the bubbling of excitement welling up inside her, she remembered Jess and the feeling leaked away, leaving her like a limp, deflated balloon.

"Don't worry, Jess will come round in the end," Mum told her sympathetically. Chloe wasn't so sure. But, in spite of that, there was no way she was prepared to give up her Big Chance. She wanted to stay friends with Jess almost more than anything, but if that were impossible, then she would choose Rockley Park every time. Did that mean she was a bad friend? Should she give up her Big Chance for Jess?

The night before the interview she spent ages washing her hair and trying to decide what to wear in the morning. If only Jess had been with her. She would have known. All week, everyone had wanted to be her friend, and yet she'd never felt so lonely. Was this what fame was going to be like? If so she was going to have to learn to be tough.

Her stomach was churning round and round. She hadn't been able to eat much tea. She tried one last practice in front of her mirror before getting into bed, but she couldn't even remember all the words to the audition song she'd chosen, though she'd been word perfect all week. It was just nerves, she told herself. She'd be fine tomorrow. She hoped. And she had to put the problems between her and Jess aside, too. For now, she had to go it alone, and do her very best by herself.

She snuggled down under the duvet and allowed the excitement to bubble back into her brain. It was going to be a fantastic experience. She would try to remember every moment, in case she was able to share it with Jess later. She probably wouldn't win a place. But she had to believe that she could do it. She had to believe that she would get a scholarship to Rockley Park, and make her dream in the mirror come true. She held that belief tightly inside her like a coiled secret.

She was so wound up she felt sure she would *never* get to sleep. She wanted to climb into her black jeans and white top, and sing. She was ready, *now*!

The bedroom door opened quietly and her mum came in. "I saw your light on. Are you all right?"

Chloe nodded. "Excited."

"Who wouldn't be? But you must get some sleep if you're going to do your best." Her mum was wearing her most worried face. "Oh, Chloe." She came and sat on the edge of the bed. "I do hope we're doing the right thing, letting you go in for this." Chloe sat up and gave her a hug.

"Don't worry," she said confidently. "It'll be all right."

Her mum sighed, and hugged her back. "You sound just like your dad," she said. "He always looks on the bright side. Oh, I nearly forgot. This came through the door for you a bit earlier." She held out a small plastic bag. "I wasn't sure whether to bring it up or leave it until the morning. As you're still awake you might as well open it now."

"What is it?"

"I don't know. Open it." Mum watched while Chloe wrestled with the sticky tape.

"It's from Jess!" Inside was a small bottle of pink, glittery nail polish. There was a note too. *Good Luck!* it said. *Love Jess.* Chloe beamed at her mum. "I've got to ring her!" she announced, scrambling out of bed. She ran downstairs in her pyjamas and dialled the number, but, of course, Jess had gone to bed.

"Tell her 'thanks ever so much'," said Chloe to Jess's mum. "And say that I'll see her very soon."

She jumped back into bed brimming full of emotion. She would wear the polish tomorrow as a talisman. It was going to be all right.

8 Rockley Park

Chloe was far too jittery to put nail polish on in the morning so she stuffed the little bottle into her jacket pocket at the last moment. Every time the excitement got too much for her she held onto it and it helped calm her down.

She'd totally forgotten that they were giving Danny, the other year-seven pupil a lift, because his mother couldn't get time off work.

"It's getting late!" Chloe fussed, as they pulled up outside his block of flats. But Danny didn't keep them waiting. He was already outside, and raced over as soon as he saw Chloe in the car.

He scrambled into the back seat with her and Ben,

clutching his drumsticks. Ben stared at him disapprovingly, alarmed at this stranger climbing into their car.

Danny was no taller than Chloe. His brown hair flopped over his face, and he didn't look anyone in the eye. Chloe caught sight of his expression and thought he looked like a frightened rabbit. Come to think of it, she probably did as well.

To begin with, Chloe's mum and dad tried chatting to Danny. *Please stop,* Chloe urged them in silence. *You're really embarrassing me.* She hunched down in her seat and tried not to listen, but it was impossible. They kept going on about Chloe wanting to be a pop singer ever since she was tiny. But Chloe had the distinct impression that Danny wasn't into pop music.

"I like Nirvana," he said, when Mum asked him who his favourite pop singer was. "They were a rock band."

"Didn't one of them die, years ago?" Chloe's dad asked.

"Yes," said Danny.

They gave up after that. Soon they were on the

motorway, and everyone went quiet. Ben fell asleep and Chloe concentrated on stopping herself from being sick with nerves. She sneaked a few glances at Danny. He was twitching and tapping in a really irritating manner. Maybe he was practising his drumming. It was making her feel even more nervous. She glared at him and he stopped for a few minutes, but was soon at it again.

Chloe took the bottle of nail polish out of her pocket and twisted the top open and closed several times. She tipped it one way and then the other, watching the gloopy pink liquid coat the inside of the glass. The polish glittered with tiny silver sparkles. She was going to be a star. She was going to sparkle. She *was*. If she could only stop feeling so sick, and scared.

Rockley Park was in the middle of nowhere. They had to stop and look at the map twice before they found it. But eventually, they were turning in through the gates and Chloe got her first glimpse of the school. It was at the end of a long, gravel drive, and looked like one of those big houses owned by the National Trust.

It was all tall windows and vast gardens. A man on a tractor was mowing the autumn grass, spraying it up into the air where it fell behind him like rain. There were lots of cars parked outside. They all looked new and shiny, not like their old heap, which had a cracked bumper because Chloe's dad had reversed into a bollard a few weeks ago.

They parked and got out. Danny and Chloe glanced at each other and away again. They didn't know each other well enough to share the excitement of the moment.

"Come on then." Chloe's dad was taking control. He led the way over the crunchy yellow gravel and in through the open door. The huge hall echoed with the voices and footsteps of the people milling about. There were signs with arrows pointing in every direction. *Music Technology* this way, *Dance Studio* that way. *Practice Rooms, Dining Room, Auditorium*. Dad went to the front desk to ask where they had to go. He found out that Danny was going to have his audition first, while Chloe had to go upstairs for her interview.

"I'll go with you, Danny, if you like," offered Chloe's dad.

"There's no need," the lady at the desk told him. "You won't be allowed in anyway. You and your wife and little boy might as well wait until the children have finished. There are magazines and drinks in the lobby. You'll be quite comfortable. Now." She looked at Danny. "You wait here for a moment. And you go upstairs, young lady, first door on the right. Give your name to the woman at the desk. Afterwards come back down here to me and I'll tell you where to go for your audition."

It was all happening too fast. Chloe wasn't ready. But Mum and Dad had already given her a good-luck hug and were going into the lobby with Ben. It was no good panicking; she was on her own now. Chloe set off across the vast hall towards the stairs. Her trainers squeaked horribly. Which door had the lady said? Chloe looked back at the desk but she was busy with someone else. Only Danny saw her.

"Good luck!" he called, his voice echoing.

"You too." Her voice was much too quiet for him to have heard. She started up the red-carpeted stairs.

She felt as if she were going to an execution, not towards her life's ambition.

There were voices above her. Some people were coming downstairs. Thank goodness; she could ask for directions now. But when Chloe saw who it was, she knew she couldn't speak to them! Bouncing down the stairs, their long dark hair streaming behind them, were the most famous twins in the country! Chloe couldn't believe it. They had been in her magazine last month, modelling clothes for the winter. They were unmistakable, with their gorgeous coffee-coloured skin and dark eyes. They were as beautiful in real life as they were in Chloe's magazine. Pop 'n' Lolly, seriously rich and famous models, coming down the same stairs Chloe was going up. They might be her age, but Chloe couldn't ask *them* anything!

At the top of the stairs a long corridor stretched away in front of her. She was wondering what to do when a voice came from the open doorway beside her.

"Name?"

"Oh!" Chloe went in gratefully. "Chloe Tompkins."

The woman ran her finger down a list, found Chloe's name and ticked it off.

"You're a singer, aren't you?" she said. "Sit down over there. They'll call you through when they're ready."

Chloe sat nervously between a girl of her age dressed all in black and a much older boy, whose knee was poking out of his jeans. She'd never been called a singer before. It made her feel as if she really might be one day!

The girl in black turned to her. Chloe smiled, although the girl didn't look very friendly.

"What are you doing for your audition piece?" the girl asked in a very posh voice.

Chloe told her shyly. "What about you?" she asked.

But the girl curled her lip in disdain. "Wouldn't you like to know?" she replied nastily. "You should never tell people in advance."

Chloe was totally crushed. She reached into her pocket and clutched the bottle of nail polish. Had she ruined her chances already?

9 The Interview

"It doesn't matter who knows about your song." It was the boy with the holey jeans. Chloe looked at him gratefully. "I'm playing *Freebird* on guitar," he added quietly. "Pay no attention to *her*."

"Chloe Tompkins? Can you come through, please?" A woman was standing at the open door. Chloe got up in a rush. She didn't see the girl's long legs, stretched out in front of her.

"Careful!" the girl yelled loudly, as Chloe tripped over them. "Mind my tights!" She drew her legs back under her and glared at Chloe as if she were a worm.

"Never mind," the woman said, as she guided Chloe into the interview room. "Don't let that unsettle you."

But Chloe was very unsettled indeed.

There were three people sitting behind a long table. They looked quite friendly, but Chloe was simply petrified. For a long moment she stared at them, frozen to the spot. Then she realized one of them had been speaking.

"Sit down," the woman in the middle said again. Chloe sat.

"I am Mrs. Sharkey, the Principal of Rockley Park School," the woman continued. "This is Mrs. O'Flannery, our medical officer. She oversees the girls' pastoral care."

Mrs. O'Flannery was really young, much younger than Mrs. Sharkey, even younger than Chloe's mum. She was wearing a dark blue uniform that made her look a bit like a nurse. She smiled, but before Chloe had even thought about smiling back Mrs. Sharkey was speaking again.

"This is Mr. Penardos, Head of Dance," she said. Chloe panicked.

"But I'm not doing dance!" she protested in a rush. "I'm doing pop singing! You must have me muddled up with someone else." For an awful moment she wondered if she'd been sent someone else's audition letter. Perhaps she shouldn't be here at all!

"Don't worry," Mr. Penardos said. "Mr. Player, he has your tape an' will see you later for your audition. This is jus' to talk." He was amused, but she could see he wasn't laughing at her. He was being friendly.

"You've just started at Beacon Comprehensive School," Mrs. Sharkey said. Chloe nodded. "What performance experience have you had up to now?" she asked.

"Well..." Chloe tried desperately to think of anything she had done. "I was Mary in the last Nativity Play at primary school, but there wasn't any singing in that."

"No carols or anything?"

Chloe blushed. "There *were* carols, but I didn't sing them." Her confession came out in a rush. "Mrs. Pendle, our teacher, always said I was showing off because my voice didn't blend in. In the end I just opened and closed my mouth as if I was singing so

I wouldn't get told off." Mrs. Sharkey and Mrs. O'Flannery exchanged glances.

"Any out of school activities? Church choir? Anything like that?" Chloe shook her head miserably. She hadn't been going to say about Mrs. Pendle. What on earth had made her do that?

"So, do you sing in secret?" asked Mr. Penardos. He wasn't teasing her. He sounded sympathetic.

"Well," admitted Chloe. "I suppose it is a *sort* of secret." Mr. Penardos made a note on the pad in front of him and smiled encouragingly.

"Go on," he said.

"Me and my friend, we *love* singing," confided Chloe. "We practise in my room all the time. But we have to be quiet because of my baby brother. We dance as well," she added, "but Mum bought me a desk for my homework, and now there isn't really enough room. Oh! And I forgot. I'm in the chorus of *Bugsy Malone*, but we haven't actually *performed* it yet. We're still rehearsing. It's going to be our Christmas production."

"Is there anything you'd like to ask us?" said Mrs. Sharkey, scribbling away on her pad.

Chloe had been prepared for this because Mr. Watkins had told her to have a few questions of her own. He'd said that she would impress them if she asked something instead of sitting there like a pudding. But she'd forgotten all the things she had been going to ask. In a moment, her chance would have gone and they would think she was completely hopeless.

"Will..."

"Yes?"

"Will... I fit in?" she blurted out. "I mean, will all the people here be rich and different from me? I mean... When I come here, will it be all right, being on a scholarship and everything?"

Mrs. Sharkey drilled her steely eyes right into Chloe's.

"At *this* school, the *only* things that matter are talent and dedication," she said. She sounded really cross. "You can't buy either of them," she went on, "however wealthy you are. And it's a matter of *if* you come here to study, not *when*, young lady. Thank you for coming, and good luck with your audition. You can send Tara Fitzgerald in now."

Chloe was on the other side of the door almost before she realized she'd got up. She'd forgotten to say thank you, or goodbye, or anything. All she knew was that she'd messed up her interview dreadfully. They would think she was useless, and big-headed too.

The boy had gone, but the girl, Tara was still there. She got up to go in for her interview but shrank away from Chloe.

"Ugh! Don't come near me." She was staring at the pocket of Chloe's dark jacket.

"What?" Chloe looked down, and there, all over one of the pockets was a bright pink stain. For a moment she couldn't imagine what it could be. She touched the colour gingerly, and her hand came away all sticky. Oh no! Jess's nail varnish!

Chloe had been twisting the top of the bottle all morning. She must have loosened it so much that the varnish had leaked out! Whatever was she going to do? And what would her mum say? This was Chloe's one and only jacket!

She had to sort herself out before her audition. But was there time? Today was turning into a terrible mess.

10 Disaster

For a moment Chloe felt really angry at Jess for giving her such a stupid present. Then she felt ashamed of herself. Of course it wasn't Jess's fault. There was only one person to blame, and that was herself.

"Here!" The woman at the desk was holding out a wodge of tissues. "You'd better go to the loo and sort yourself out."

Chloe grabbed the tissues gratefully and held them to the sticky mess. Forgetting to ask for directions she dodged out of the room and headed down the empty corridor. Where, oh where, was the loo? She had to get there soon or she would leave a trail of vivid pink glittery drops all over the floor.

At last, someone appeared round the corner. He was a big man, quite old, with greying dreadlocks, his scruffy trainers making no sound on the carpet. Chloe always hated asking anyone where the loo was. She felt she would die of embarrassment. But she had no choice. She simply *must* do something with her jacket.

"Excuse me," she said. "Can you tell me where the ladies is?" She had the sort of lump in her throat you get when you're trying not to cry, so she didn't speak very clearly.

"Sure," he said in a relaxed voice once she'd asked him again. "Straight along, down the stairs, through the swing door to your right and it's the red door on your left." He didn't seem to notice her distress or the problem with her jacket.

Chloe shot along the corridor and down the stairs. She pushed through the red door into the ladies and took a deep breath. She almost felt as if she were drowning.

The tissues were sticking to her jacket, and her hands were sticky too. Chloe didn't know what to do for the best. A couple of older girls were fixing their hair at the mirror and they moved so she could get to the sink.

"Oh no! What's happened to *you*?" one of them asked.

"What's that on your jacket?"

Chloe would rather have been by herself. She was still having trouble with the lump in her throat, but she couldn't be rude.

"Nail polish," she mumbled, pulling at the mess of tissues to throw them away.

The girls were really kind. They did their best. But there wasn't much *anyone* could have done without nail polish remover, and no one had any of that. Water was no use at all. They helped her out of the jacket and held it while she reached gingerly into the pocket to put the top on properly. They made suggestions while she tried to clean her hands. Then, the best they could do was to cover the stain with layers of paper towels and fold the jacket up with the stain inside so the rest of her clothes would stay clean. All this time, the lump in Chloe's throat was getting bigger and bigger. But she couldn't afford to hang around. She had to get to her audition, even if she still had sticky hands. She was certain now she'd never be able to sing a note.

Carrying the jacket carefully, she headed for the door. As she reached it, Tara pushed it open from the other side. She stared at Chloe for a moment.

"Oh! It's clumsy clogs," she said. "Mind out of the way, stupid!"

Chloe sidled past her, feeling tears pricking her eyes. Was Tara this horrible to everyone? But there was no time to feel sorry for herself. She had to report back to the lady at the entrance hall for her audition. She headed down a corridor, through a swing door and down some stairs. This wasn't right!

A large group of practically grown-up dancers came towards her, all sweaty T-shirts and loose trousers. They were talking loudly, and laughing at each other's jokes. Chloe shrank against the wall of the narrow corridor to let them past. She couldn't ask them the way. The lump in her throat was so big she couldn't ask anyone *anything.*

Once they'd gone, she sprinted along the corridor, looking desperately for a way out. A door to one side looked promising, but then she saw the red light above it, and a notice saying: *No entry when red light is on.*

Chloe kept going, and eventually came to a short flight of stone steps. To her astonishment, at the top of the steps she found herself back in the entrance hall. Thankfully she went over to the desk.

"Ah, Chloe Tompkins," the woman said. "Mr. Player has been waiting for you. You're late. Through there. It's the door marked *Voice Coach.* Hurry up."

A couple of seconds later, Chloe was in the audition room, swallowing desperately to get rid of the huge lump in her throat.

"This is Mrs. Jones, who will be your accompanist, and I am Jeremy Player, the voice coach." Mr. Player didn't look as if he were annoyed at having to wait. The woman at the piano smiled slightly at Chloe and then looked away.

"Have you been running?" asked Mr. Player. Chloe nodded.

"Well then, take a moment before we start," he said. "You can put your jacket on that chair." Chloe laid the jacket gingerly on the velvet-covered chair, and readjusted a paper towel that was threatening to fall out.

"Ready?"

Chloe wanted to say no. She wanted to explain about the lump, and the jacket, and the fear she felt seeping into her very bones, but she couldn't. The lump wouldn't let her speak at all, so she simply nodded. Mr. Player turned to the pianist and she began.

Chloe tried. She really tried, but the notes ran away from her and she couldn't catch up. She came in late, her breathing was awful, and all the time the lump in her throat was getting worse and worse. Mr. Player shook his head and looked at Chloe regretfully.

"I have to verify that the voice sent in on the tape is really yours," he said. "I'm sure it is, but you're so nervous you're not giving me your best. Would you like to try again?"

So they tried again, but it was almost as bad. Then they went on to the scales. They were a little better, but nothing like as good as when she'd sung them for Mr. Watkins. Chloe knew she was letting herself down. She knew she would do much better if only the lump would melt. If only she hadn't fiddled with Jess's present and ruined her jacket. If only everything hadn't gone wrong almost from the moment she had arrived.

At last it was over.

"Maybe you're not cut out for this kind of thing," Mr. Player said kindly. "Not everyone can perform solo, even if they *have* got great potential. Don't let your parents force you into performing if you don't want to. Join a choir instead. It's much less scary than singing solo."

He waited while she fumbled to collect her jacket, and then held the door open for her. As she left, he patted her kindly on the shoulder.

"Never mind, Chloe. Thank you for coming. Goodbye."

Chloe stumbled out and round the corner. Straight

ahead of her a door stood wide open, with the autumn sun streaming in. She gave a choking sob, ran outside and slumped, miserably, onto the ground.

11 A Friend in Need

"Hey! How you doin'?" Chloe looked up. It was the man with the greying dreadlocks again, standing in the doorway. "Hey," he said again, his smile fading. "It can't be as bad as that. What's up?"

Chloe couldn't help it. She just burst into tears. And then it all came tumbling out. About how she'd wanted to be a pop singer for so long and about her Big Chance and how she'd ruined it. The nail polish present that had spoiled her jacket, and getting lost, and worst of all not being able to sing because of the lump in her throat.

"Everything has gone wrong," she told him between hiccuping sobs. "Mr. Player thinks I don't really *want* to sing. He told me not to let my parents push me into it. But it was *them* who wanted to stop *me*!" She was crying so hard it was a wonder he could make out anything she said.

"Here," he said, handing her a huge blue hanky. "Can I join you?" She nodded and he put the carrier bag he was holding on the ground and eased himself down with a grunt. "I eat my lunch here most days," he told her. "Though I usually favour the bench."

Chloe looked to where he was pointing and saw an old wooden bench. She felt guilty that he was sitting on the flagstones on her account, but he didn't seem to mind. He was leaning back against the wall, his wrinkled, brown face turned up to the pale patch of blue sky above. Once she'd blown into the hanky a few times, it was very quiet in the sunny little courtyard.

"Why d'you want to be a pop singer so much, anyhow?" he asked.

"I've *always* wanted to," Chloe sniffed, wiping her nose.

"But why? Wantin' to isn't an answer."

A Friend in Need

She sniffed again. No one had ever asked her why before. She thought hard about what he'd asked.

"So I can be famous I suppose," she said at last. It didn't seem a very good reason once she'd said it, but he didn't laugh at her. He just asked another question.

"And why d'you want to be famous so much?"

She leaned against the wall like him. It was warm against her back. She thought about all the things she could have if she were famous. She thought of flying round the world, staying in big hotels, earning loads of money and having people cheer and clap when she went anywhere. She did want all those things, but she wanted something else much more.

"I want people to *like* it when I sing," she said. "I don't want them to say I'm showing off like they did at my last school. I want them to really like it. I want to make people happy when I sing."

He turned and looked at her. He really was quite an old man, with wrinkles and lines scribbled all over his face. But his eyes were different. They looked young somehow. They were full of fire and they lit up his face.

"I know what you mean," he said quietly. "Makin' music is a very fine thing. But you don't have to be famous to do it."

"I do," said Chloe. Then she explained about her room, and Ben and about the teacher who had stopped her from singing naturally.

"That teacher must have been one jealous old coot," he said. That made Chloe laugh and cry at the same time and she had to blow her nose again.

"What song did you sing today?" he asked at last, when she had recovered herself a bit.

She told him sadly. His laugh was a huge guffaw of merriment.

"Why, man, that's one crazy song!" he said, grinning broadly at her. "It's not my kind of music at all. Why d'you want to sing that?"

"I don't know," Chloe sniffed. She tried to be annoyed but his laughter was so infectious she couldn't. "Jess thought it was a good idea."

"The way I see it is," he went on, "you got so het up, no way could you sing, however good your voice is.

But I'm sure those tears have melted that lump in your throat. Isn't that so? Reckon you could sing that song now?"

He hummed the tune quietly, one hand tapping out the time on his knee. He might not like the song but he certainly knew it. His whole body was moving with the rhythm and Chloe found it easy to join in. To her surprise, the lump in her throat was completely gone. He nodded at her and grinned and they finished the song together.

"Do you think Mr. Player will still be there?" Chloe asked him eagerly. She felt so much better, she was sure she'd be able to sing properly for him now.

The old man shook his grey dreadlocks. "I don' know. D'you want us to find out?"

Chloe nodded. If only she could have another chance. She *knew* she wouldn't make a mess of it this time.

"Here!" He took a packet of sandwiches out of the carrier bag and handed the bag to her. "You put your jacket in there."

He struggled to his feet and they went back to the

audition room together. He had just raised his hand to knock when the door opened and the lady who'd played the piano came out.

"Hello, Jim," she said to the old man. "Do you want Jeremy? He's still here. You've just caught him." She smiled at Chloe and hurried away down the corridor.

"Jeremy!" Jim put his arm round Chloe and brought her with him into the room. Mr. Player turned round from the piano, where he'd been stacking paperwork. "Are you going for lunch?" he asked, and then paused, noticing Chloe. "Is there a problem?" he added.

"Not really," said Jim in a cheerful voice, "but this young lady had a few disasters before she sang to you, and she wondered if she could have another chance."

Chloe held her breath. If only he would say yes. She was sure she'd be able to sing beautifully for him now.

"Well... What's your name?" Chloe told him and Mr. Player shuffled through his papers. "Yes, here it is. You're one of the ones from Beacon Comprehensive, aren't you? No previous experience of performing... Tompkins, Chloe. That's you, isn't it?"

Chloe nodded furiously.

"I remember. You were the one that sang scales on the recording."

"Yes," she agreed.

"Well, come here." He went round to the piano keyboard and played a chord. "Sing these scales quickly for me."

Chloe did as he asked. He didn't tell her to stop when she was finding it difficult, and Chloe did her best to keep going, but in the end she was forced to stop.

"Okay," he said, when she'd sung as high and as low as she possibly could. "I don't have time to listen to your audition song again now, but I know it's on your school recording. I'll listen to it again later. That's the best I can do."

"Thank you," said Chloe, trying to stop her voice from wobbling. She didn't mind singing scales, but it was hardly a performance, and her voice had squeaked embarrassingly on the last couple of high notes.

"You're welcome. Now if you'll excuse me…"

"Thanks, Jeremy," Jim added, steering Chloe towards the door. "I'll catch you later."

As soon as they were out of the door, she turned to face him. She was going to thank him, but he waved her thanks aside.

"Now don' you fret," he said. "You can't make things come right every time. But you've had another chance now, and you can be sure there will be others. You have a fine voice, and I can see you're determined enough to get there in the end. You're one of those brave people who get up and fight again after they've been knocked down. Isn't that so?" Chloe nodded. No way was she going to let herself cry again. Not if he thought she was brave.

"What does the teacher in your new school say?" he asked.

"He says I should join the choir. And he's let me be in the chorus of *Bugsy Malone*," she told him, trying hard to look on the bright side.

"Well, I would say that's a good start," the old man said. "I began in my school choir many years ago, before I had my first guitar. It might not always be your sort of music but it's better than none. And *Bugsy*, I know that! You'll have fun doing Mr. Bugsy Malone, and you won't get spoiled in a school production."

"What do you mean?"

He looked down at her and smiled, but he looked sad. "Well, I've seen so many people in this business spoiled by fame," he said. "Good people some of them, who couldn't handle the money, or the attention and wrecked their lives because of it. I've had friends who started off like you, wantin' to make music. By the time they'd finished, they didn't know what they wanted any more. They ended up ruined by drink, drugs, or fast livin'. They got lost along the way, Chloe." He sighed.

"This is a fine school, and they work hard at keepin' the kids on the straight 'n' narrow. But it's a tough business to survive in. It's easy to forget that however famous you become, you're still the same, ordinary person inside. Don't leave your old friends behind if you do get famous. They are the ones who will keep you sane because they know who you really are." He smiled again. "It's been fun singin' with you, Chloe Tompkins. Enjoy *Bugsy Malone* now, won't you?"

Chloe offered him his hanky back but he just looked at it and laughed. "Reckon it's more yours than mine now," he said. "You keep it to remind you of the fun we had singin' that crazy song together." He took her hand, sticky as it was, and shook it, as if she were an adult. Then he turned, and left Chloe alone, feeling empty and hollow inside, but somehow calm and comforted too.

12 Diamond Days

Chloe wandered back to the entrance hall deep in thought. The old man was probably right. Maybe there *would* be other chances. After all, not *every* famous pop singer had been to Rockley Park School.

There was a guided tour of the school before they went home. Chloe didn't really feel like going on it, but she knew she'd regret it if she didn't go. They trailed round in a large group, and were shown classrooms, the dining room, the dance studio and even one of the bright, cheerful bedrooms where the students slept. Chloe was so fascinated she almost forgot that she'd failed her audition. Most exciting of all was the room Chloe had passed with the red warning light outside. The light was needed because down that short passage was the school's very own recording studio!

Chloe squeezed into the control room with the others. Through the glass panel behind the mixing desk she could see a rock band setting up. They had one little room for the drum kit and another for the guitarists. There were cables trailing everywhere and all the musicians had headphones on. The mixing desk looked *so* complicated. There were rows and rows of knobs, and several computer screens too. A grey-haired man in a cardigan and wearing headphones was twiddling the knobs and talking to himself.

"Give me some snare, Joe," he'd say. Or, "Floor tom. Steady beat." Chloe hadn't a clue what was going on, but she could have stayed there all day.

"This is Mr. Timms, our recording engineer and Head of Music Technology," said the boy who was showing them round. Mr. Timms took off his headphones and swivelled his chair to face his visitors.

"I'm doing sound checks at the moment," he said.

"But I can show you how we record music on lots of different tracks and then put them all together. Here, each of the black lines shows a sound picked up by a different microphone." He pointed to where lots of lines were running slowly across a computer screen.

"It's like the monitors you see in hospital dramas on telly!" said a girl at the back of the room. Everyone laughed, but Mr. Timms nodded.

"Very similar," he agreed. "The lines on hospital monitors jump whenever there is a heartbeat. Here they jump when there is a drumbeat. Look. Give me a bit of snare again," he said into a microphone set into the mixing desk. So he wasn't talking to himself after all! He had been talking to the drummer in the studio. As the boy hit a drum, one of the lines on the screen jumped up and down.

"There you are," said Mr. Timms. "Now, I have five different microphones on those drums. Each one will pick up a different sound and the sounds will be recorded separately. Now, listen to this." They all watched while he twiddled several knobs. The lines disappeared for a moment. When they came back, they were all jumping and jerking on the screen.

"This is a recording I made awhile ago," Mr. Timms explained. "Ten microphones were used, so you can see ten separate lines jumping. With these sliders on the mixing desk I can bring in whichever sound I like, however softly or loudly I need it."

It was amazing! When all the sounds were turned up, Chloe could hear a band playing with drums, guitars and two singers. As he slid the knobs, different sounds were taken away until Mr. Timms was left with one of the guitars all on its own. It was brilliant. Chloe wished she could have a go.

"Those of you who get a place at this school will learn how to mix the music you make," Mr. Timms said. "Understanding recording techniques is an important part of making music in the twenty-first century."

As the group made their way back out of the studio, they passed Chloe's friend with the dreadlocks. He was waiting to go into the control room.

"Hey! Chloe," he said, grinning at her as if they'd

been friends for ever. "How y'doin', kid?" Chloe grinned back.

"Fine," she said. "Thanks."

Several of the kids looked at her enviously and once they were out of the studio one said, "How do you know *him*?"

"We got talking." Chloe shrugged, not wanting to admit how upset she'd been.

"Lucky you!" said a girl she'd seen earlier who had been carrying a guitar.

"Why?" Chloe asked. The girl stared at her.

"Don't you know who he is?" she asked. Chloe shook her head. "He's only Judge Jim Henson!" the girl said. "He's Head of the Rock Department! I was scared stiff doing my audition in front of him. He's performed with loads of awesome people in his time!"

"Oh!" Chloe said. "Well, he's really nice."

Before everyone went home, they filed into the small theatre, where Mrs. Sharkey, the Principal, was waiting to speak to them.

"Only a few of you will be accepted as students

here," she said. "But I don't want any of you to go home feeling failures. You *all* have something to offer, otherwise we wouldn't have called you for interview."

Chloe perked up at that. They must have thought she had *something* about her then. And she wouldn't be the only one to go home disappointed. She hadn't thought about loads of the others being rejected too.

"You all have ambitions," Mrs. Sharkey continued. "And, whatever they are, you must hold on to them with all your strength. Being a success in the music industry is one dream that many people will tell you is impossible to achieve. But never you mind if no one at home takes your ambitions seriously. Never mind if you don't know anyone else who has achieved what you want to achieve." Chloe listened carefully.

"Maybe you won't make it," Mrs. Sharkey admitted. "There is a risk of that in *every* career choice. But you don't want to worry about that now. You are just at the beginning of your lives. These are your Diamond Days, when anything can happen. Walk towards your dream every day with a sparkle in your eye. Don't worry if you don't know the way. Trust your heart to lead you and you won't go far wrong. Thank you all for coming, and I wish you all the very best."

Chloe filed out with the others.

"How did you get on?" Danny asked her as they met in the main hall.

She shrugged. "Not very well," she told him reluctantly. "How about you?"

"I don't know," he said. "It was scary. Come on," he added, "let's go and find your parents."

Chloe wanted to stay positive on the way home, but it wasn't easy. Mrs. Sharkey might well be right about Diamond Days, but not only had Chloe ruined her Big Chance, now she also had to face her mum about her ruined jacket!

13 Waiting

Chloe managed to avoid letting on about her jacket on the way home, but once they had dropped Danny off and come indoors she couldn't keep it a secret any longer.

"Honestly!" her mum exploded when she saw the mess the jacket was in. "What were you thinking of, carrying nail polish in your pocket all day? That was a really silly thing to do." Chloe could feel tears seeping out of her eyes.

Her mum sighed, put the jacket down and folded Chloe in her arms. Chloe wished she were a little girl again, and could sit on her mum's lap. She hugged her back instead.

"Sorry," she mumbled.

"Come on. You're overtired, and overemotional," Mum said. "It's been a long day. Don't cry. We all do silly things sometimes. I've got a new bottle of nail polish remover in the bathroom. Bring it down and we'll have a go at getting the polish out."

Chloe still didn't feel like talking about the audition, but now she was home her mum and dad wanted to hear all about it. Bit by bit, the whole sorry tale came out. Chloe's mum and dad did what they could to help her to make the best of it.

"Fancy Judge Jim Henson helping you out," Dad said. "I've always loved his music. What an experience you've had!"

"That's right," Mum agreed. "No one can take that away from you. It's been a day you'll always remember."

That was certainly true.

The next day was Saturday, and Jess came round. Chloe had been looking forward to seeing her so much, but at first they were very awkward with each other.

"I meant you to *wear* the polish, not carry it round in the bottle," Jess said when Chloe told her about the accident.

"Sorry," Chloe said. For a few moments there was silence.

"It's all right," said Jess. And suddenly everything *was* all right between them again.

It helped that Chloe didn't have anything to crow about. They put some music on, and while it played Chloe told Jess all about her disaster of a day at Rockley Park.

"I'm *so* glad we're friends again," she added. "It was horrible when you wouldn't speak to me."

"I was just so jealous," Jess admitted. "I tried to tell myself it was all your fault that I hadn't got an interview, but of course it wasn't. Mr. Watkins must have been right about singing scales. I'm glad he didn't ask me to do it. I could never have sung them like you did. Anyway, I'm sorry you messed up the day, but I'm glad we're still going to be going to school together.

And you know, I'm not sure I'd really *want* to be a pop singer any more."

"Why not?" Chloe was amazed.

"Well, you had a horrible time yesterday, didn't you? And we stopped being friends for a bit. It must be so difficult being famous. Besides, I don't think I'd want to go to school away from home. Mum would be lonely all on her own. Anyway..." She grinned at Chloe. "We'll be in *Bugsy* together now, if you haven't got in to Rockley Park, and that'll be a real laugh!"

"S'pose."

"Come on," Jess urged, going over to Chloe's wardrobe and opening it. "Let's have a fashion show!"

Jess and Chloe's fashion shows were almost as much fun as pretending to be pop stars. They roped Ben in as usual, and dressed him up in scarves, hats, and so many bangles he rattled. He loved it, especially when they let him put some sparkly make-up on his nose.

But Chloe's mind was only half on their game. She was trying to remember everything Mrs. Sharkey had said about her Diamond Days. She *wouldn't* forget to walk with a sparkle in her eye. And no way was she ready to give up on her ambition yet. In spite of everything that had happened she was just as ambitious as she had always been.

It was hard, terribly hard waiting to hear that there was no place for her. Because, until Chloe heard one way or the other, a tiny part of her still insisted on hoping. She knew it was stupid after the mess she'd made of the interview and audition, but she couldn't settle until she knew for certain.

So every day Chloe pounced on the post before leaving for school, only to be disappointed. Every day, that is, until one morning, a week after the interview, when she was running late.

She was shovelling down her cereal as quickly as she could. Jess would be dawdling at the end of the road, wondering if she was sick. Chloe hoped she'd wait, or come and knock at the door. She hated walking to school on her own. Besides, this morning she wanted to ask Jess about their history homework.

She still had to finish her breakfast, brush her teeth, put on her shoes and coat and walk up the road. So, when she heard the post slide through the letterbox, she groaned. There was no time to look at it *this* morning. Ben toddled off to pick up the letters instead. He liked to pretend he was a postman and insisted on giving everyone, including his teddy, a letter. This morning, Chloe got a double-glazing advert perched on the edge of her bowl.

"For oo."

"Ben!" Chloe complained, as the corner slid into her milk. "I don't have time for this."

She shoved her bowl into the sink and raced off to clean her teeth. While she was sitting on the bottom of the stairs doing up her shoes, he dumped another one on her laces.

"For oo."

Chloe brushed it off impatiently and it slid with a crisp, expensive whisper to the floor. She looked at it. She could hear Ben chattering away, back in the kitchen, but it was quiet in the hall. She picked up the letter and held it. She could tell where it had come from.

She told herself it wouldn't be so bad not getting in to Rockley Park. *Bugsy* was fun. And Mr. Watkins had told her she could sing as loudly as she wanted. He really loved her voice.

She'd have a different Big Chance some other time, maybe when she was grown up. It was most likely all for the best.

She finished tying her laces and put on her coat. If she hurried, she'd probably still catch Jess.

"Chloe?" Her mum and dad were peering out of the kitchen at her. Goodness knows how long they'd been there. "Well?" her mum said.

"Oh!" said Chloe in a rush, scrambling to her feet and handing her mum the letter. "I must go. Don't worry. It's all right. I don't mind too much. I'll be all right, really." Her heart was suddenly pumping away, beating so loudly she was sure her parents must be able to hear it.

"But you haven't opened it!" her mum said to Chloe, holding the letter out.

"I know!" she said, sniffing. "I know what it says. I must go." Tears were sliding down her cheeks. She did mind. Of course she did. She minded terribly. She'd been telling herself all week that it didn't matter, but it did. It mattered more than anything else in the world.

"Chloe!" Mum called after her. "Open it, won't you?" Chloe was crying too hard to answer so she just shook her head and opened the front door. Jess was coming up the front path.

"What's the matter?" she asked, seeing Chloe's blotchy face.

"Chloe!" Dad was calling her back. She must have forgotten her bag, she was in such a state. But it wasn't her bag.

"Chloe." He shoved the opened letter at her. "You've got in, you silly girl!"

Chloe looked at Jess but her eyes were all fogged up with tears and she couldn't see.

"I've got in!" she cried.

14 Well Done

Chloe Tompkins seemed to be doing a lot of crying.

She'd always thought it was stupid that people cried when they were happy. Now she realized you couldn't always help it. She should have been able to stop her tears when she heard the news, but they just kept flowing! Her dad put his arms around her and lifted her off the ground in a big bear hug, but instead of giggling as usual when he did that she cried even more. She was really cross she was doing it but she still couldn't stop.

They all went back into the kitchen and sat down at the table. Chloe was a jumbled mess of tangled thoughts. She just couldn't get herself together. She kept laughing and crying at the same time. In the end she just gave up trying to control herself. She let all the tears shoot down her cheeks and drip onto the table. It was amazing how big the puddles got.

Everyone else was talking. Jess had come in as well, and the kettle was coming up to the boil. It felt to Chloe as if she were somewhere else, listening to them from a long way off.

After leaving her to cry in peace for a few minutes, Chloe's mum wiped the tears off the table and put a mug of tea in front of her. Then she quietly wrapped her arms around her daughter. Chloe leaned against her mum. She sniffed, her dad handed her a tissue and her mum loosened her hug a little while she wiped her nose. And then she hugged her again.

"It's the shock," she said calmly. "Don't worry. It'll pass off in a moment." It *was* passing off, but Chloe felt exhausted, even though it was morning and she hadn't been up for long.

"We are *so* proud of you," Dad said. "Here, try sipping some tea. It'll help." Chloe looked round, but Jess wasn't there.

"Where's Jess?" she asked in a wobbly voice.

"She had to go," Mum said. "She said she'd see you at break."

"I'll be late for school."

"I'll be late for work!" said Dad. "I must go, love. But we'll celebrate properly tonight. I can't wait to tell my mates. What a daughter I've got!"

Once Dad had gone, Chloe noticed Ben standing by the door, staring at her with his thumb in his mouth. She patted her lap. "Come on," she said. "It's all right."

"He wonders what's going on," Mum said as Ben clambered up. He busied himself trying to fit the letter back in its envelope while Chloe gave him a cuddle.

"I'm going to be a pop star," she told him in a small voice. When she said it, it sounded true for the very first time. Somehow, saying it made it real.

She couldn't stay sitting any longer. She put Ben down and stood up. It was impossible to keep still now the truth was sinking in. She walked up and down the kitchen, letting the excitement flood through her. She had got in! Thank goodness Judge Jim Henson had calmed her down. She would never have been able to approach Mr. Player again if Judge Jim hadn't helped. She owed him a huge thank you.

She was really going to Rockley Park! She would learn how to be a proper singer. If she did really well, she would sing on television and at concerts. She would be famous! A huge smile was stretching over her face. She couldn't help it. She picked up the letter and read it for herself.

I have pleasure in offering a full scholarship place at Rockley Park School to Chloe Tompkins. Please reply immediately if you wish your daughter to accept her place. Full details of term dates and items needed are enclosed. If you have any problems, or questions, please don't hesitate to phone Mrs. O'Flannery, who will do her utmost to help.

"You are going to let me go, aren't you?" she asked, suddenly worried. Her mum nodded.

"I wouldn't fancy our chances if we tried to stop you!" she said. "Having had a look at the school, and met some of the teachers, I think it's a wonderful opportunity. Of course you can go."

Chloe set out for school once she'd washed her face. Afterwards, she couldn't remember walking. She thought she must have floated there. She'd missed assembly and half of English but Mr. Morgan wasn't at all cross.

"Come in and sit down, Chloe," he said. "Jess explained why you would be late. Congratulations, by the way!"

After the lesson, loads of people wanted to know all about it. It was nice feeling like a celebrity but Chloe wanted to talk to Jess. She didn't want to risk her best friend becoming upset again. Judge Jim Henson had been right when he'd told her how important old friends were.

"It's okay," Jess said, once everyone had left them in peace at last. She swung her school bag at Chloe to make her point. "Just make sure you don't forget me! And make sure you come and see me in the holidays," she added. "I want you to remember what it was like before you were famous!"

"Of course I will," Chloe promised. Judge Jim Henson had said that too.

The next thing Chloe had to do was find Danny James. As she'd had her letter this morning, maybe he'd had his too. No one seemed to know, but then Danny James didn't talk much, as Chloe and her parents had discovered on the journey to Rockley Park.

Chloe didn't consider herself Danny's friend, but she found herself hoping that he'd been accepted as well. It would be comforting to have *one* face she knew, even if he was a boy, and a drummer rather than a singer.

Eventually she caught up with him just before the bell went after lunch. He was mooching along the corridor by the hall, tapping out a rhythm on the wall.

"Hey!" Chloe called, as he was about to disappear round the corner. "Danny!" He stopped and waited for her to catch up.

"What?"

"Have you got your letter yet?" she asked.

"Heard you did," he replied. It was impossible to tell how he felt about that.

"But have *you*?" Chloe asked again. She *really* wanted him to have got a place now. They might even be in the same class for some lessons.

"Yeah," he said. "I got a letter."

"Well?" She held her breath.

"Reckon I'll see you there," he said, a slow smile spreading over his face.

15 Nearly There

There was a lot to think about. Chloe wouldn't need a uniform, but there was a list of suggested clothes she might like to take with her. For sport and dance classes, Rockley Park recommended their own jogging trousers and shirts, and an order form was enclosed.

"That's good!" Chloe's mum said in relief after worrying at the prices. "Mrs. O'Flannery has put a note in to say not to buy the sports kit new. Look! She says there's a thriving second-hand shop at the school and she's sure they'll have your size." Chloe wasn't too sure about that. She didn't want everyone to think she was from a poor family, but she knew that there wasn't much money for extra clothes, especially as her parents had only recently kitted her out for Beacon Comp.

There were forms to fill in and her room to sort out and tidy before she left. Jess sat on the bed and went through all the things Chloe had decided to throw out.

"Can I have this pencil case?" she asked. "And are you sure you don't want that blue Indian scarf?"

"Nah. It's got a hole in it."

"I don't mind. I like it." Jess sat with the scarf in her lap, looking rather sad. That was unlike her, she was usually so upbeat. "I'm going to really miss you, Chloe," she said, scrumpling the scarf into a ball. "You *won't* forget me, will you?"

Chloe gave Jess a big hug. "I'll miss you too. And I'll *always* want to see you, Jess. I promise."

These were definitely Chloe's Diamond Days. She walked around with a sparkle in her eye; even when she was being told she must do her homework, as it would never be marked, because soon she'd be at a different school!

She knew she still had a long, long way to go before she achieved her ambition, to sing to the thousands of fans in her imagination. But she'd had a Big Chance, she'd taken it, and now she was walking in the right direction.

She knew that there would be loads of difficult times ahead. And sometimes it was scary, the thought of changing her life so much. Some nights she lay in bed worrying about what was to come. Would anyone like her? Had Tara got a place, and if so would she make Chloe's life a misery? Sometimes Chloe wondered if she would be homesick, and wish she'd never *heard* of Rockley Park School.

She wouldn't be able to go home every weekend. So while Jess was out shopping with friends, what would Chloe be doing? Would she be stuck there in the country, working every hour of every day? And what about her voice? Would she be good enough? And if she couldn't fit in at Rockley Park, what then? How could she ever go back to Beacon Comprehensive? It would be awful to have to go back as a failure. But most of the time, Chloe felt nothing but excitement. She stuck to her determination to stay a good friend to Jess.

"We can text each other once Dad has got a mobile for me," Chloe told Jess a couple of days before she was due to leave.

"Yeah!" agreed Jess. "You can tell me all your news, and I'll do the same. You must give me all the gossip, too, so I can let the others know at school. Everyone will want to hear how you're getting on.

"I'm going to be so popular!" she added with a grin. "It'll be as good as being a famous pop star without all the hard work!"

Chloe giggled. "I hope Dad gets me a phone that can take pictures too. If he does, I'll send you a shot of me in my school bedroom."

The night before Chloe left for Rockley Park, Jess came round for tea. After tea they went up to Chloe's room, where two large suitcases stood waiting by the door.

"This is for you," Chloe said, pulling a small parcel out from under her pillow.

"What is it?"

"Open it and see!"

Jess pulled at the wrapping while Chloe stood waiting, suddenly feeling shy.

Inside was a framed photograph of them both. Chloe's dad had taken it last Christmas, when the girls had been dressed up, pretending to be their favourite pop stars.

"Do you like it?"

Jess threw her arms around Chloe and hugged her. "I love it!"

"I've got one just the same, to take with me," Chloe explained. "I wanted to give you something to say thank you for being my best friend."

"I can't believe you're going away tomorrow," said Jess, looking at the picture.

Chloe nodded. "I know! But, look, I'll be back before you know it. My term is shorter than yours because I'll have lessons on Saturdays. And I'll get one weekend at home before the Christmas holidays. We'll have good fun this Christmas. For a start, I should be home in time to see you in *Bugsy*! We'll have so much to talk about!"

It was really hard saying goodbye. Chloe and her dad took Jess back home in the car because it was late. Chloe and Jess didn't know what to say, so they just hugged. Then Jess simply waved briefly and vanished indoors. Chloe was very quiet on the way home, but her dad understood and left her to her own thoughts.

Back in her room, Chloe sat at her dressing table, staring into the mirror. For some reason, the crowd of fans she could usually conjure up in her mind refused to appear. It was as if she were just offstage, waiting for the signal to go on. The fans were there, *would* be there when the time was right, but for now she was content to wait. She had a lot of work to do, a lot of things to learn.

So many people had helped her get this far. Jess, and Mr. Watkins, even her mum and dad were being helpful now. And Judge Jim Henson must have helped the most of all, for her to get her place at Rockley Park.

"But now," she told her reflection firmly, "now, it's up to me!"

✸ So you want
to be a pop star?

✸

Turn the page to read some top tips
on how to make your dreams
✸ come true... ✸

✴ Making it in the music biz ✴

Think you've got tons of talent?
Well, music maestro Judge Jim Henson,
Head of Rock at top talent academy Rockley
Park, has put together his hot tips to help
you become a superstar...

✴ Number One Rule: Be positive!
You've got to believe in yourself.

✴ Be active! Join your school choir
or form your own band.

✴ Be different! Don't be afraid to stand
out from the crowd.

✴ Be determined! Work hard and stay focused.

✴ Be creative! Try writing your own material –
it will say something unique about you.

✴ Be patient! Don't give up if things
don't happen overnight.

✴ Be ready to seize opportunities
when they come along.

✳ Be versatile! Don't have a one-track mind – try out new things and gain as many skills as you can.

✳ Be passionate! Don't be afraid to show some emotion in your performance.

✳ Be sure to watch, listen and learn all the time.

✳ Be willing to help others. You'll learn more that way.

✳ Be smart! Don't neglect your school work.

✳ Be cool and don't get big-headed! Everyone needs friends, so don't leave them behind.

✳ Always stay true to yourself.

✳ And finally, and most importantly, enjoy what you do!

Go for it! It's all up to you now...

Usborne Quicklinks

For links to exciting websites where you can find out more about becoming a pop star and even practise your singing with online karaoke, go to the Usborne Quicklinks Website at www.usborne-quicklinks.com and enter the keywords "fame school".

Internet safety

When using the Internet make sure you follow these safety guidelines:

* Ask an adult's permission before using the Internet.

* Never give out personal information, such as your name, address or telephone number.

* If a website asks you to type in your name or email address, check with an adult first.

* If you receive an email from someone you don't know, do not reply to it.

For another fix of

read

Rising Star

1 New School

The limousine swished past the wrought-iron gates and up the drive. It drew to a halt with a crunch of gravel outside the impressive front entrance. Chloe got out to the cheers of her fans, who had waited all day to see their favourite pop star.

Well, it was a nice thought. But today's reality wasn't quite as exciting as Chloe's daydream. There *were* plenty of cool cars arriving at Rockley Park School, but Chloe's family owned a rather old Vauxhall with a cracked bumper, not a limousine. Never mind. One day the dream might come true. After all, this was only Chloe's first day at her new school. Winning a scholarship to this very special place *might* be the first step to pop stardom. Because, as well as all the usual lessons, this school taught everything that a singer needed to know!

Rockley Park was a school for aspiring pop stars, songwriters and musicians. It was full of students who were really talented and determined to get to the top. Here, Chloe would get all the voice training she needed, as well as learning how to dance, record her own songs, and all the technical stuff she would need for a career in the music industry.

Chloe peered out of the car. Her dad had followed the signs, and pulled up outside a new building at the back of beautiful old Rockley Park House. This was Paddock House, where all the year seven and year eight girls slept. A long row of windows looked out over the car park and the fields beyond. One of those windows might be Chloe's room…

"Well," said Mum. "We're here." Chloe's little brother Ben had been asleep, but as Chloe opened the door and scrambled out, he woke up.

"Me too," he demanded, and Chloe leaned in to undo his seat harness.

"Don't let him run off," Mum warned. "You know what he's like." But Ben was still too sleepy to run anywhere. He stuck his thumb in his mouth and watched some people nearby unloading a large trunk from the back of a four-wheel-drive. Chloe wished she could have a trunk, but they were far too expensive – her family just couldn't afford one. Dad opened the boot and took out the shabby suitcase they'd packed Chloe's belongings in. Chloe grabbed two full carrier bags and Mum picked up Ben.

Chloe had been waiting impatiently for this day ever since she'd found out that she'd won a scholarship. But now she'd arrived she had mixed feelings. Thank goodness Danny James, a drummer from her old school, had won a place as well. At least there would be *one* face here she would recognize.

"Excited?" asked Dad. Chloe nodded, but it certainly wasn't just excitement she was feeling. There was a whole cloud of butterflies fluttering about in her stomach and a lot of unanswered questions in her head. Would she be homesick? Would she be able to make friends? Would she find the school work too difficult? Most important of all, was she a good enough singer to make it to the top?

A woman with dark, curly hair was at the front door.

"Welcome to Paddock House," she said, shaking hands with Chloe and her parents. "You are… ?" she asked Chloe cheerfully.

"Chloe Tompkins."

"Right, Chloe. I'm Mrs. Pinto, your housemistress. Any problems or worries, you come to me, and if you don't want to do that Mrs. O'Flannery over in the health centre will sort you out." She checked the list she was holding. "Now, your room is on the first floor, at the end of the corridor. There will be four of you in there, all year sevens, of course. Come along. I'll show you the way."

Chloe's family all traipsed along behind Mrs. Pinto.

It was chaotic in the house. There were lots of fire doors that were stiff to open, and the stairs and corridors were full of other girls and their parents, all loaded with belongings, trying to squeeze past each other. You could tell the new girls easily. They were the ones that looked lost, with harassed parents attached. The older girls were much more lively. They greeted each other with squeals of delight and got in the way of everyone else by hugging each other enthusiastically.

"*Do* move out of the way, girls," Mrs. Pinto told a group of four chattering together excitedly. "Go and get some tea if you've unpacked. You can catch up with all your news in the dining room."

Eventually, Mrs. Pinto opened yet another door and stood aside to let Chloe and her family in.

"Here you are," she said. "It looks as if the two beds by the window have already been taken, so choose which one you'd like on the other side and get settled in. Tea is in the dining room in the main house when you're ready. I usually suggest that parents say goodbye here," she said to Chloe's mum. "Do come into the kitchen downstairs for a cup of tea with the rest of the parents, though, before you head for home. It's on the right by the front door."

"Do you want us to help you unpack?" asked Chloe's mum once Mrs. Pinto had gone.

"No, thanks," said Chloe.

Dad could see how she felt. "Come on," he said to his wife, who was hovering around, looking helpless. "Chloe needs to sort herself out. I expect her new roommates will be back soon. Hey! Don't do that," he added, going over to Ben. Chloe's little brother was jumping up and down on one of the beds by the window. "That belongs to some other famous pop star."

"Dad! No one here will be famous for years and years," Chloe said.

To find out what happens next read

Cindy Jefferies' varied career has included being a Venetian-mask maker and a video DJ. Cindy decided to write *Fame School* after experiencing the ups and downs of her children, who have all been involved in the music business. Her insight into the lives of wannabe pop stars and her own musical background means that Cindy knows how exciting and demanding the quest for fame and fortune can be.

Cindy lives on a farm in Gloucestershire, where the animal noises, roaring tractors and rehearsals of Stitch, her son's indie-rock band, all help her write!

To find out more about Cindy Jefferies, visit her website: www.cindyjefferies.co.uk